Tails of Jaxx at the Metropolitan Opera

TAILS OF
JAXX
AT THE
Metropolitan
Opera

Joanna Lee Doster

MPI
PUBLISHING

Publisher: MPI Publishing
ISBN-13: 978-0-9960179-2-3
ISBN-10: 0996017925
Library of Congress Control Number: 2015919728
Cover and interior design: One of a Kind Covers
Visit Joanna's website at:
http://authorjdoster.wix.com/joannaleedoster
First Edition

Contents

Dedication

This story is dedicated to my beloved Maltese dog, Jumping Jack Flash, an animal actor who has always loved people, the stage, bright lights and applause. Fearless, talented and brave, he has never missed a cue in life or while performing in operas at The Metropolitan Opera at Lincoln Center in New York City.

The adventure, *TAILS OF JAXX AT THE METROPOLITAN OPERA* was inspired by Jack's real life performing experiences at The Metropolitan Opera from 2007 to 2010, where he came to be known affectionately as "Jacques the Opera Dog." He performed in the operas *War and Peace* by Sergei Prokofiev, *Manon Lescaut* by Giacomo Puccini and in *Der Rosenkavalier* by Richard Strauss, where he appeared with the renowned legendary American opera singer, Renée Fleming.

He was also featured in the 2009 EMI DVD *Manon Lescaut* with Karita Mattila.

"Jack was a wonderful colleague in *Der Rosenkavalier*, and I'm so happy that he has inspired this charming story that features a lovable dog and opera – two of my favorite things in the world." - Renée Fleming

1

Chapter One

FANCY GOLDEN CURTAINS OPEN UP in front of me. Dazzling bunches of brilliant colored lights twinkle in my eyes as they light up the stage. I try to look through the bright lights out into the audience. It's too dark to see any of their faces, but I hear the murmur of people's voices.

It's opening night and I'm all tingly. Even the loud music played by the musicians hidden below in the orchestra pit thrills me. I love hearing the wonderful sounds coming from violins, and trumpets, flutes, and cymbals.

I wiggle excitedly in my friend Leonardo's arms as he carries me to our special place onstage, next to my horse friends, Apollo and Zeus. I am dressed in a vibrant red velvet coat and my hair has been brushed to a silky gloss. I remember to remain quiet and still, just like Leonardo and I practiced in rehearsals. Leonardo, singing in his deep, baritone voice, guides me to the famous opera singer Melisande, and puts me on her lap. A glowing spotlight shines on her beautiful face. She's my friend, too. She begins to sing the pretty song I heard her sing yesterday, during the opera's big rehearsal.

Oh, no! My tummy is doing somersaults.

But then, Apollo, looks at me as if to say, "A piece of cake. Just calm down."

It's my first day as an actor under the bright lights of The Metropolitan Opera.

My name is Jumping Jaxx, and I am a seven year old Maltese dog.

How did I ever get here?

2

Chapter Two

I T ALL BEGAN TWENTY-FIVE DAYS AGO on a cold, blustery Saturday in February. I live in an apartment house with my parents in New York City. It's the best city in the world, especially for a dog like me.

Saturdays are my favorite days. I get to spend the whole day alone with my daddy. We go to the dry cleaners, then to the newspaper store where the nice owner, Mr. Theo, always has a biscuit for me. Sometimes we go the drugstore to buy toothpaste or shampoo, or to Daddy's office nearby. The last thing we always do is head over to our special dog run in Central Park. There my daddy lets me run around and play with my favorite dog friends, Mackenzie and Parker. Our favorite game is Nip-The-Tail-On-The-Doggie!

On that particular Saturday, on the way home, my daddy said, "Jaxx, we have to make one more stop to pick up roses for Mommy." He draped my leash around a bicycle stand. "Wait. I'll be right back." Then, he patted my head.

I lay down, and listened to the city noises; the hubbub of taxicabs honking their horns, the zipping of cars, trucks and buses in and out of traffic, and the startling sounds of sirens that make everyone move out of the way. My favorite New York City sound is the clop-clop-clopping of the horse's hooves against the rough pavement as they lead their horse-drawn carriages along Central Park.

I saw lots of people dashing about on foot, weaving in and around the cars and cabs and I wondered where everyone was rushing off to.

All of a sudden, the sky turned dark and angry. It began to snow very hard. I curled into a ball and watched the door where Daddy went in.

Why hasn't he come out yet?

WHOOSH!

A powerful gust of wind whipped through the air. The next thing I knew, I was propelled down the street and my blue collar and leash went flying off my neck. It landed in the middle of the road, just as a gigantic city bus went whizzing by.

CRUNCH!

The wheels of the big bus crushed and dragged and smooshed my leash.

WHOOSH!

Freezing blasts of cold air sent me flying down another street. I landed on all four paws and hit the ground hard.

Heavy snowflakes were pouring down faster

and faster. Everything was covered in a blanket of white.

OH, NO! Where am I? My dad never took me here before.

People were holding on to their hats. It seemed as if they were floating by. Every time I tried to get up, the driving winds would knock me down again. I could hardly open my eyes to see clearly, the wet flakes kept sticking to them. I was so frightened and cold.

This was not at all like our usual Saturdays. Was I having a scary dream?

I wanted my daddy.

WHOOOOOOSHH!

The raging storm threw me against a big building.

I huddled in a corner, chilled to the bone and scared. My paws hurt and were stinging me. I began to shiver and cry.

"O-ww-oo-ohh!"

A squeaky door opened. I didn't dare move.

Icy sharp winds whipped around my face and I howled, "Arr-oo-ow!"

"WHO'S OUT THERE?" someone shouted.

The crunching sounds of snow, underneath someone's heavy footsteps, were getting closer.

Then, a big hand scooped me up. I could tell by the way he held me, he wasn't my daddy.

Oh no! Who was this stranger?

3

Chapter Three

"WELL, HELLO THERE, LITTLE BUDDY."
The big man gently brushed the snow and ice off of me.

"Are you lost?"

He looked at me with friendly eyes.

"Why, you're quite a handsome fella."

I was frightened out of my mind, but he was wearing a badge on his jacket like the one the security guard wears at my dad's office building.

"You don't have a collar on, do you?"

He held me up.

"Nope. No collar, no tags—no nothing. Well, let's go inside and get out of this storm. You can stay with me until we find out who you belong to, okay?"

Before I could wiggle out of his arms—*never go with strangers, never go with strangers,* he carried me inside to a big room and climbed up into his booth. He put me on his lap and picked up the phone.

"This is Clarence," he said. "I found a cold, wet pup."

Br-r-r-r!!

I was shivering.

"Francesca, do you think you might have something warm to wrap him up in?"

A few minutes later, a pretty lady appeared

with a blanket. She also held a red sparkly collar and leash.

Francesca kissed Clarence on the cheek. She smiled at me, "Oh, mon garçon doux, vous êtes si beau." She patted my head. "Let Francesca take care of you."

She leaned in and kissed me too. She smelled like flowers. I whimpered because I didn't know where I was, or who these people were. I missed my mommy and daddy so much!

"Oh, mon petit garçon, don't cry. I found something for you from the costumes I work on. Here—let me dry you off."

She wrapped me up in a warm blanket. It felt so nice and soft, just like my mom's fluffy coat. Her sweet voice calmed me down, and I felt better.

"Do you have time to take our little friend down to the cafeteria?" Clarence said. "He must be starving."

"Mais bien sûr," she replied.

Francesca lifted me off Clarence's lap and said. "Oh my, you must be thirsty and hungry."

My tummy started to growl. Francesca carried me down many, many steps to the cafeteria. The yummy smells made my stomach growl even more.

Francesca gave me some food and water. It was scrumptious and I gobbled down everything. I couldn't remember what she fed me but my tummy was full and I got all warm inside.

I must have fallen asleep. I don't remember Francesca bringing me back. When I awakened, she and Clarence were chatting. Clarence scratched me behind my ears and said, "You'll stay here with us, little buddy, until we find your owners." He turned to Francesca. "I'll be working double shifts for a while. I'll watch the dog until I leave in the morning. Would you be able to take care of him during the day?"

"Bien sûr, Clarence. I can do that," she said.

"Hmmm," said Clarence, "What should we call him?"

"He is so handsome and brave," she said. "How about Valentin?"

"Or maybe—Valentino," said Clarence.

"Oui! That's better! Valentino!"

I curled up on a big pillow Clarence gave me. I felt safe here with my new friends.

Yet, as I drifted off to sleep, I wondered...

Would I ever see my mom and dad again?

4

Chapter Four

WHEN I WOKE UP THE NEXT MORNING, my stomach went into a knot. I slowly opened my eyes and sniffed.

This doesn't smell like my house. Where am I?

Then I remembered, I was lost and Clarence had rescued me. I quickly looked up.

Oh, good. He's here.

Clarence leaned over and pressed a buzzer to open the security door. Francesca walked in.

"Bonjour, mes amis. How are you, Valentino?"

She hugged me.

Clarence stood up and said, "I'm leaving now. See you later, Valentino." He rubbed me behind my ears, just like my daddy does. I didn't want Clarence to leave. I wiggled out of Francesca's arms and chased after him.

"Oo-oooo," I wailed.

Was I was going to lose him, too?

Clarence kneeled down and patted my head. "I'll be back later, Valentino. I promise."

Francesca caught up to me and said, "Valentino, let's go for a walk outside before it snows again. Okay, mon cher?"

We were across the street when I heard a familiar bark. I saw my dog-friend Mackenzie walking with his mom, Grace.

"Arf! Arf! Arf!"

Mackenzie! Grace! It's me, Jaxx! I'm here!

I had to catch up with them to let them know where I was. I ran as fast as I could dragging Francesca behind me, trying to avoid the deep piles of snow. But it was too late. Mackenzie and Grace had turned the corner and disappeared.

Now my parents would never find me!

"Valentino, who were you chasing? Francesca said. "We almost fell!"

"Oh-h, mon cher! Look at the time. I have to start work!"

I met Francesca's assistant, Freddie. He had a nice face. He was all fidgety and spoke very fast, but I liked him.

They brought me to the wardrobe room. Freddie talked a lot while he kept busy. He told me that Francesca was the wardrobe mistress for the opera house and that he worked with her. He said that she made costumes for the singers, dancers, actors, and even for the animals. I didn't have a clue what Freddie was talking about, but I did notice that Francesca sat at a sewing machine most of the time.

They made a nice comfy spot on the floor for me with big fluffy pillows. Strangers kept coming into the room looking through rows and rows of colorful clothes on many metal racks to see what they liked. Then they would go to the back room to try them on. It reminded me of the stores my mom would take me to when she would go shopping.

Maybe the opera house is a place where people party, sing and dance, and even find clothes to wear?

My daily routine was the same. After my morning walk and breakfast, I'd take a nap. Once, when I was about to doze off, a cat scooted right past me. The hair on the scruff of my neck stood up. Francesca saw him, too.

"Valentino, that is Caramelo. He lives in the opera house to keep away the mice."

After my morning nap, it was time to go to work! I followed Freddie around all day while he helped people choose their costumes and made sure they fit.

The opera house was as large as a New York City block. We walked down long hallways, passing by a lot of rooms where people worked. They would wave to me and call me Valentino instead of my name Jaxx, but I barked "hello" back at them anyway.

5

Chapter Five

MY DAYS WERE FUN, BUT THE NIGHT time made me lonely, scared and sad. I missed my parents so much. I had been living at the opera house for over a week, when...

BOOM—BOOM—BOOM!

The pounding sound of loud drums coming

from the orchestra late one night echoed throughout the building. I awoke to my own terrified barking.

It brought back a horrible memory.

When I was very small, just a little puppy really, my daddy took me for a walk. Out of nowhere, a booming bolt of lightning ripped through the sky. Twisted branches of white crackling bursts of light illuminated the sky. We both practically jumped out of our skins. I shook and trembled all over.

After that, whenever thunderstorms rolled through, I would hide under the bed and shake. One day, my parent's good friend, Grace, invited us over. She had heard about my thunder-phobia and knew how to cure it. It had worked for her dog Mackenzie, my play pal.

"This song is for Jaxx," she said. "It's called *Minuetto*, from my favorite opera. It always calms Mackenzie down when he's frightened."

It worked. From then on, whenever my parents played *Minuetto* for me during thunderstorms, I would calm down.

BOOM—BOOM—BOOM!

Another loud drum sound shook the place again. Clarence heard me cry out and put me on his lap.

"There, there, Valentino. Everything will be all right."

He rubbed me behind my ears and held me until I fell back to sleep.

Another day, as I made my rounds, I heard my favorite New York City sound of the clop-clop-clopping of horse's hooves getting closer. I looked up and saw a huge horse head lean down.

He was so big, he scared me at first. But then, he greeted me warmly and said, "I heard you were new here and I wanted to meet you."

"Oh, hello! They call me Valentino, but my real name is Jaxx. I lost my tags, collar and everything. I got separated from my dad during a terrible snowstorm, but Clarence rescued me. What's your name?"

The big horse shook his mane and let out a snort. "Whew! You sure have been through a lot!

I'm Apollo. I'm an actor here at the opera house." Apollo nodded over my head and said, "Let me introduce you to my other animal friends."

First, I met Zeus. Apollo told me that sometimes he and Zeus pulled a big carriage onstage. Then, I met some animals I had never seen before; some goats, rabbits, and birds in cages.

"Come visit us whenever you want," Apollo said.

And that's how Apollo became my good friend.

6

Chapter Six

FREDDIE AND I WERE DOING OUR errands, when Caramelo, the cat, signaled me to follow him. He led me near the stage where the singers and dancers were rehearsing.

Wow! The lights, the costumes, the music. It gave me goosebumps!

Caramelo nudged me. "See that lady singer? She loves dogs. You should say hi."

I ran to her, sat down and wagged my tail very hard. She smiled, and sang right to me!

"STOP! Stop the music!" a lady shouted from offstage. "Freddie! Get that dog out of here—NOW!"

Freddie rushed onstage and lifted me into his arms. "Sorry, Kathryn. It won't happen again."

Out of the corner of my eye, I saw Caramelo strutting away with his tail up in the air.

"Valentino!" Freddie whispered sternly. You're not allowed to be on the stage."

He took me to a quiet area as we watched the opera together.

"Valentino, this is where the operas are performed. Operas are like plays, but instead of people talking to one another, they sing. Opera singers have the most beautiful voices."

Freddie pointed to the singers under the brightly lit area. "See, Valentino? They perform on a big stage facing the audience. It's like a movie theater or place where people go to hear concerts. The orchestra is hidden below."

Then he took me backstage. There were singers, dancers, actors and I recognized some of the animals. Everyone waited until it was their turn to perform.

Even though I was living in the famous Metropolitan Opera in New York City, I was homesick.

Would I ever sleep in my own bed again?

7

Chapter Seven

*B*ANG—BANG—BANG!

A week later when Freddie and I were making our deliveries, I heard a loud thumping noise.

BANG—BANG—BANG!

I turned to Freddie, but he must have taken off.

BANG—BANG—BANG!

I ran closer to the sound. It was coming from the special holding pens for Apollo and Zeus. The door was closed.

BANG—BANG—BANG!

"Apollo, it's me, Jaxx. What's wrong?"

"Oh, thank goodness," he cried. "There's a mouse in between my hooves driving me crazy! Can you get someone to open the door?"

"Hang in there! I'll go get Freddie! Is Zeus in there with you?"

"No," said Apollo. "He was taken out earlier to be groomed."

I raced back to the wardrobe room and found Freddie.

"Arf! Arf! Arf!"

"Not now, Valentino! Freddie scolded. "Stop that barking! I'm fitting Arlene's costume!"

I barked louder and pulled on Freddie's pant cuffs.

"Valentino, stop that!"

I ran to the doorway and then back to Freddie. "Arf! Arf! Arf!"

BANG—BANG—BANG!

Just then, Freddie heard the noise, too. He followed me to Apollo's pen.

BANG—BANG—BANG!

"Neigh-h-h-h!"

"Help! I need help!" Freddie yelled. "A horse is in trouble!"

Freddie and a stagehand let Apollo out. The stagehand got rid of the pesky mouse.

Apollo snorted in relief. "Thanks, Jaxx."

I stayed with Apollo while he calmed down.

"I don't know how a mouse got in here," said Apollo.

"Isn't it Caramelo's job to get rid of mice?"

Where was he?

8

Chapter Eight

"♫ *LA-LA-LA-LA-LA-LA-LA!* ♫"

Freddie and I were taking costumes to one of the singers, when I heard it.

"♫ *LA-LA-LA-LA-LA-LA-LA!* ♫"

I peeked in a room and there was the nice lady from the stage the day before. When she spotted me, she stopped.

"Oh, Freddie! Is this the same cute dog from yesterday? Is he yours?"

"Yes, Melisande. He's the same dog, but no, he doesn't belong to me. He was lost during the last snowstorm and we don't know who he belongs to. So, we're watching him while we search for his owners. In the meantime, he's become part of our family here."

"Well, he's absolutely charming. Does he have a name?"

"We call him Valentino."

Freddie looked at me and said, "Valentino, this is Melisande, the famous opera singer."

Melisande smiled. "Would it be all right if he kept me company while I rehearsed?"

"Yes, of course," said Freddie. He patted me on the head. "Valentino, stay with Melisande and be a good boy!"

My ears perked up when Melisande began to sing. Her song reminded me of the one Mommy and Daddy used to play for me whenever I was scared. It made me a little sad, because I missed being at home with them very much. But I loved it and that made me happy again.

As I pranced and danced around the room, I spotted something shiny on the floor. I picked it up and tossed it around a few times.

Melisande stopped singing. "Valentino, what are you playing with?" She came over to look. "Oh Valentino, it's my lucky diamond pin! You found it! It must have fallen off my dressing table. My beloved mother gave it to me for luck."

Melisande pinned it on her dress. "My dear Valentino, you're my lucky charm, now." And then she hugged me.

If I never found my mom again, could Melisande be my new mom?

9

Chapter Nine

I T'S FUNNY HOW MY STAGE CAREER BEGAN.
"Melisande," I overheard Kathryn, the
director, say, "Richelieu is sick. We need another
dog actor for the opera."

Melisande pointed to me. "Valentino! He's
perfect and so handsome. Let's give him a try!"

Kathryn eyed me doubtfully. "I don't know..."

"We should ask Leonardo," said Melisande.
"He's the one who has to handle the dog."

She walked over to a very big man.

Leonardo bowed down on one knee to Melisande and kissed her hand.

Melisande smiled. "Leonardo, I would like you to meet my dear friend, Valentino, the Maltese."

Puzzled, Leonardo looked at her and bellowed, "WHO?"

"Valentino! Richelieu, the dog actor is ill. I think Valentino would be perfect to take his place. What do you think?"

Leonardo stood up. *Oh, my! He looked like a giant!*

"BRING THAT MUTT OVER TO ME!" he roared.

My ears went back and I trembled. Melisande handed me to him.

He had a fuzzy beard and was gruffer than my dad, wider than my dad, and scarier than thunder.

Leonardo frowned as he lifted me up and looked me over this way and that. My tummy did flip-flops. He slowly crouched down and set me on the floor. When he held out his hand, I was scared, but I licked it.

"BWA-HAA-HAA! HE LIKES ME," Leonardo shouted. He picked me up again in his great, big

arms and laughed, "Melisande, he's a fine boy!
He'll be perfect!"

The giant man wasn't so scary after all!

10

Chapter Ten

*O*W-W-W!
I had to sit still for a very long time. That was hard to do! Francesca was grooming me before my first rehearsal. After my hair was washed and dried, Francesca brushed me over and over for several hours to make sure my hair looked smooth and shiny.

Ouch! I had a lot of knots and they hurt!

"Oh, my dear Valentino. You are being so brave. Hold still for one more minute, my sweet. We are nearly done."

When she was finished, she hugged me.

"You are so handsome!" she said. "Wait until everybody sees you!"

She held up her mirror.

"Look, mon chéri."

Wow! Was that me?

Freddie walked in and smiled. "Look at you, Valentino!"

I looked different, but felt the same.

I wagged my tail, proudly.

Freddie took me to a great big room where the rehearsals were held. All my friends were there.

Leonardo came to get me. "Hello my little friend," he bellowed. "It's time to get ready."

Freddie whispered to me, "You're an actor, now. Your job is to be very quiet and to listen to Kathryn, the director."

I was getting very excited.

Kathryn pointed to Leonardo and said, "Remember to walk Valentino over to Apollo and Zeus and wait. When you hear the orchestra start to play *Bashert*, that will be your cue. You sing while carrying Valentino to Melisande and place him on her lap. Valentino, when he places you there, I want you to sit up and puff out your chest."

"Okay everybody!" said Kathryn. "Let's keep it moving. We have a lot to go over!"

The rehearsal lasted for several hours. I was about to doze off from all of the excitement, when my ears perked up. Melisande began to sing my favorite song. It made me so happy. I tried to imagine being onstage with her on opening night.

After Melisande finished singing, Kathryn made an announcement.

"Good work, everyone. We're through for today. Tomorrow, we'll rehearse again but this time in costumes for the formal dress rehearsal!"

Yay!

11

Chapter Eleven

"**M**E-E-OW-W!"
  Swat—Swat—Swat!

On the way back from rehearsal, Freddie and I saw Kurt the janitor swat a cat with his broom.

"You miserable cat! Get out of here!"

"Me-e-ow-w!"

"You never listen. Where's that pin?"

"Hey Kurt!" Freddie scolded. "What's the matter with you? Haven't you ever heard the expression 'Be kind to animals?' Stop that right now!"

"Aw, mind yer own beeswax!" Kurt snarled.

He was swatting at Caramelo! I jumped out of Freddie's arms and nipped at Kurt's pant legs, so Caramelo could escape. Before Freddie could drag me away, I got in a few last nips!

Kurt shook his broom at us. "Take your little fluffy muff and get out of here!

"You leave that cat alone and don't you dare harm a hair on Valentino."

The hair on the scruff of my neck was standing up. "Gr-r-r-r!"

"You better control that dog or he'll get his! Now, get out of here!"

Kurt looked around and said, "Where's that darn cat? Now you see what you did? He got away."

Freddie went back to work and I went to find Caramelo to warn him. I searched until I found him hiding behind a crate.

"Caramelo," I whispered. "It's me, Jaxx. I just wanted to make sure you're okay."

"Get away from me," Caramelo hissed. "I ain't had no family my whole life, so don't try and save me. Kurt is all I got."

"I want to help you, Caramelo. I didn't like the way Kurt was treating you!"

"Look kid, I might as well level with you," said Caramelo. "I steal things for Kurt so he'll feed me. I don't want to do it, but he makes me. When I was trying to steal Melisande's diamond pin, you and Freddie came into her room. I panicked and dropped it. I feel bad enough what I did to Apollo."

"What did you do to Apollo?"

"Kurt made me drop a mouse into his stall."

"How could you do that to him?"

"It was to cause a commotion. When everyone ran to check on the horse, Kurt was stealing stuff. Now, beat it, before he sees us talking!"

My heart was pumping so loudly in my chest. I had never met anyone like Caramelo and I felt both sad and scared for him.

"Why does Kurt steal things?"

"Easy! He sells the stuff for a lot of money. I'll let you in on a big secret. Kurt stashes all the stolen stuff in his utility closet. He keeps it hidden with his mops and pails."

We both heard a door slam.

"Hey, you better go! It's him!"

Caramelo scampered off to another hiding place.

Kurt's loud voice soon filled the backstage. He yelled, "Where are you, you rotten cat? Wait 'til I find you!"

I went running back to the wardrobe room. I saw Freddie talking very fast to Francesca. He was walking in circles, as he always does when he has something on his mind.

I barked as loudly as I could! "Arf! Arf! Arf! Arf! Arf! Arf!"

Freddie stopped talking and said, "What's wrong?"

"Arf! Arf! Arf!"

I ran back and forth to get his attention. This time Freddie knew to follow me. He rushed out the door after me.

I sprinted down the hallway and Freddie followed. I ran fast, but kept checking back to make sure Freddie was right behind me. And he was. I had to go up a lot of stairs and then down a few long hallways and then we heard the loud noises. They were coming from inside the closet.

Caramelo was hissing! My heart was racing so fast I thought it was going to pop right out of my chest.

Freddie spoke into his phone, "Francesca, tell Clarence to meet us at the janitor's utility closet. And hurry!"

Freddie, do something, quick! "Arf! Arf! Arf!"

Freddie pounded on the closet door. "Open up, Kurt! Open this door, immediately!"

Kurt was in a rage. "Beat it!" he yelled back from inside the closet. Suddenly, there was a loud crashing sound against the door.

I raced over to Kurt's closet and scratched and pawed at the door frantically.

"Arf! Arf! Arf!"

Clarence and Francesca came running. Clarence moved me to the side and kicked in the closet door. Poor Caramelo was crouched in the corner, not moving. He had put up a good fight and was all scratched up. Freddie and I ran over to Caramelo. Freddie picked him up and gently held him.

Clarence searched the closet. They found Kurt's stash of missing furs, jewelry, paintings, and much more. The police were called and Kurt was handcuffed and taken away.

"I'm going to take Caramelo to the Animal Hospital, Freddie said, I hope he makes it."

Before he left, Freddie turned to me. "Valentino, you were a hero tonight! You helped catch a thief! Good boy!

"Arf! Arf! Arf!"

I jumped up on Freddie's leg to look at Caramelo.

"See you later, my friend," I whispered to him.

12

Chapter Twelve

*K*ABOOM—KABOOM—KABOOM!
My heart was beating so fast. It was opening night. We were all dressed up in our beautiful costumes. There was so much excitement in the air. The orchestra was playing. The bright lights were shining. It felt like a dream.

My new friends Melisande, Leonardo, and Apollo and Zeus, and I were onstage.

Was I really an actor at The Metropolitan Opera?

I was so happy.

If only my parents could see me now!

Leonardo carried me over to Melisande as he sang to her, and placed me on her lap. Then she began to sing *Minuetto*, and I fell in love with her even more.

Sometimes I would sneak a glance out into the audience, but it was just too dark to see. My job was to stay focused until the opera was over, just like we had rehearsed.

When the opera ended, the curtains closed and the cast gathered together in a line. When the curtains reopened, the house lights went on.

Wow! So many people!

Melisande, and Leonardo, with me in his arms, took their bows. Then, the other singers, actors, and dancers took their bows.

Some of the people brought bouquets of roses on stage and gave them to Melisande.

"Bravo! Bravo!" the audience shouted as they stood up and applauded.

"Bravo, Jaxx! Bravo, Jaxx!" someone nearby shouted.

What?

My ears perked up and I listened harder over all the shouts.

"Bravo! Bravo!" the audience roared!

"Bravo, Jaxx!"

That sounded like...

I looked out again.

My parents! They're here! Right in the front row!

My heart was beating so loud, I thought everyone could hear it. At that moment, everything stood still. I couldn't believe it was really them. Our eyes locked.

I jumped out of Leonardo's arms and ran to the steps at the side of the stage that led out to the audience.

"Arf! Arf! Arf!"

I leaped into my dad's arms. My heart was bursting! I was over-the-moon! My mom and dad were crying with joy, and wouldn't stop hugging and kissing me.

I licked them and I licked them and I licked them!

An usher came and escorted us through the

doors that led to backstage. All of my friends were there.

They all shouted, "Hip-Hip-Hooray for Valentino! Hip-Hip-Hooray for Valentino!" Everyone was happy to finally meet my mom and dad.

Clarence lifted me into his arms. "Valentino, Francesca and I put up 'Found Dog' signs all over the neighborhood, hoping someone would come forward to claim you. This morning your mom spotted one of our signs and called. We told her you had become our opera dog and asked if she and your dad could hold off seeing you until your performance tonight."

My mom said, choking back tears, "Clarence, you will never know how grateful we are for saving our little boy. And thank you, Francesca. Clarence told us what a wonderful job you and Freddie did taking care of our Jaxx. It's a miracle! After searching day and night for so long, we were losing hope. Thank goodness you took him in and kept him safe."

Clarence and I looked at each other. We really didn't have to say anything. We both knew we would always be forever-friends. Then he patted me behind my ears, just like he always does. *How do I thank the man who saved my life?*

Francesca's eyes were all wet. "Mon chéri, Freddie and I made you a special gift." She pulled out a black velvet cape that had white embroidered letters that said 'Valentino The Opera Dog,' and tied it around me. "This is so you'll never forget you are our Valentino."

She put up her mirror for me to see and I strutted around looking at myself.

It smelled so familiar. Could it be? Yes, the cape had been made from the blanket Francesca had wrapped me up in the night I was rescued.

Kathryn introduced herself to my parents. "Valentino is a pure delight. He has become a great part of the opera house. He is a very talented dog, who has proven how special he is. The Metropolitan Opera would be honored to employ him as an animal actor for as long as he would like."

My father said to her, "Well, Kathryn, if Jaxx, I mean Valentino, wants to perform..."

He looked at mom and she nodded 'yes.'

"...then, we'd be pleased to have him be a part of the opera house."

Oh, boy! Oh, boy!

I wiggled and danced all over and ran up to

each of my friends. I knew I would be able to see Apollo and Zeus whenever I wanted.

Melisande picked me up and whispered, "Remember, Valentino, you shall always be my lucky charm."

I licked her face and she began to cry.

Freddie came in holding Caramelo. He greeted everyone and announced that Caramelo, was feeling much better.

'"From now on, I'll be taking care of him."

Wow! Caramelo!

He looked uncomfortable, but happy. Something was different about him... He smelled clean! And he was wearing a sparkly collar!

"Caramelo, is that really you?"

He said to me, "P-s-s-t! Jaxx... It was Freddie's idea. How am I going to keep up my tough cat image wearing this collar? At least I won't have to steal diamonds anymore."

"I'm so happy you're okay."

"Um, Jaxx, I wanted to thank you for saving me from Kurt. Freddie is very good to me. I ain't never had three squares and a nice warm bed, but I'll get used to it."

Freddie was chatting with my parents. "...and we'll have play dates and get-togethers."

Both Caramelo and I laughed.

"As Apollo would say, 'A piece of cake,' after what we have been through."

The last thing I remember that night was getting into a taxi cab with my parents. With all of the excitement, I must have fallen asleep. When I awoke and opened my eyes, I could smell I was truly home.

Home! I could hardly believe it! All my things were still where I remember. My toys, my tattered old blue and red blanket. My horseshoe shaped, blue velvet bed. Oh, my own bed.

Dad tucked me in. "Good night, Jaxx," he said, and gave me a big, long, hug.

Mom kissed my forehead. "We love you for forever and a day!"

I licked them back.

As I drifted off to sleep, I thought about all my adventures at The Metropolitan Opera.

And then quietly, I whispered, *Good night, Clarence.*

Glossary of French Terms

Chapter Three
Oh, mon garçon doux, vous êtes si beau! – Oh, my sweet boy, you are so handsome!
Oh, mon petit garçon – Oh, my little boy
Mais bien sûr – But, of course
Bien sûr – Sure
Oui – Yes
Chapter Four
Bonjour, mes amis – Good morning, my friends
mon cher – my dear
Chapter Ten
mon chéri – my darling

About the Author

Joanna Lee Doster, published author of *Maximum Speed: Pushing The Limit,* (MPI) and *Celebrity Bedroom Retreats*, (Rockport), is also a freelance journalist for syndicated newspapers, (Gannett), magazines, (Millimeter) and blogs. She has held executive positions in communications, worked for television production companies and for cable television programming networks such as: Arts & Entertainment, The Learning Channel and PBS. She lives in New York.

Acknowledgements

My deepest gratitude to:
Linda Chiara, my extraordinary editor, for her expert guidance.
Ashley Fontainne, of One of a Kind Covers, for her brilliant designs and creative vision.
Ken Howard, photographer, The Metropolitan Opera, for his beautiful pictures of Jack's performances.
Nancy and Paul Novograd of All Tame Animals, Jack's wonderful talent management, who offered him the golden opportunity to perform at The Metropolitan Opera.
John Monteleone, Jack's amazing animal trainer.
All the very talented men and women at The Metropolitan Opera, who were so gracious in sharing their magical world with Jack.

To my beloved husband for his love and inspiration.

Special thanks to the following for their unwavering support and friendship:
Lucy and Peter Ascoli; Wendy and Peter Bernstein; Rosemarie Brower; Dr. Bonnie Brown; Arlene and Tom Buckley; Niamh Clune; Pat Conner; Chris and Lou Cook; Marsha Casper Cook; Johnine Cummings; Sara and Charles Dossick; Betty Dravis; Haesook Han; Chloe and Elyse Harbert; Donelda Hawley; Dr. Pia Hiekkaranta; Dr. Jeffrey Hubsher; Dr. David Kellman; Debbie Kerner; Susan King; Lloyd Korn; Mia and Stanford Kravitz; Cyndy Landgraver; Marcia Madeira; Marley Egan Maier; Skyler Egan Miller; Nancy Mizels; Roberta Parry; Ashley Poitras; Erin, Steve, and William Reardon; Yonatan Tsapira; Chanel J. Tucker; Diane Vaillancourt; Sally J. Walker; Helen Weber; and Krissy Weiser.

Credits

I wish to thank the following illustrators and providers whose contributions helped make this story come to life:

Der Rosenkavalier: Photo by Ken Howard.

The Metropolitan Opera at Lincoln Center: Photo by Blehgoaway.

Can Stock Photo Inc.: Dazdraperma; olgaov; Annapisanets.

Stage on cover: Designed by Freepik

Shutterstock.com: McCarony; Sarunyu_foto; karakotsva; IvanNikulin; Jacky Brown; Subarashi21; Pushkin; Andreas Meyer; Clipart design; Dennis Cox.

Vecteezy.com: Nicole Lind.